by **BETTY COMDEN** and **ADOLPH GREEN**

What's New at the Zoo?

with an introduction by **PHYLLIS NEWMAN**

illustrations by **TRAVIS FOSTER**

Blue Apple Books

Published in the United States 2011 by
Blue Apple Books, 515 Valley Street, Maplewood, NJ 07040
www.blueapplebooks.com
First Edition   07/11   Printed in Dongguan, China
ISBN: 978-1-60905-088-7

2 4 6 8 10 9 7 5 3 1

Introduction

On December 26, 1960 a big Broadway hit musical, "DO RE MI," was born at the St. James Theatre in New York City.

from left:
Jule Styne, Betty Comden, Adolph Green

The words in this book are the actual lyrics of a song from that show, and were written by the iconic team of Betty Comden and my husband, Adolph Green. The music was composed by the brilliant Jule Styne.

On January 11th, just sixteen days after the show opened, another Broadway baby was born, our first child . . . a son. A few years later, our daughter joined us. We went to the zoo a lot. We loved those animals. We sympathized with their plight. And now, your kids who are, and your babies to come—EVERYBODY—can enjoy and find out *What's New At The Zoo!*

— Phyllis Newman
Tony award-winning actress

to the **bear** said the **kangaroo.**

The **seal** flipped his FLIPPERS, swallowed several kippers . . .

then they all began to chant:

said the goose to the tall **giraffe.**

THAT's what is new at the zoo!

Hey Bill!

"You're stepping on my QUILL!"

said the porcupine to the swine.

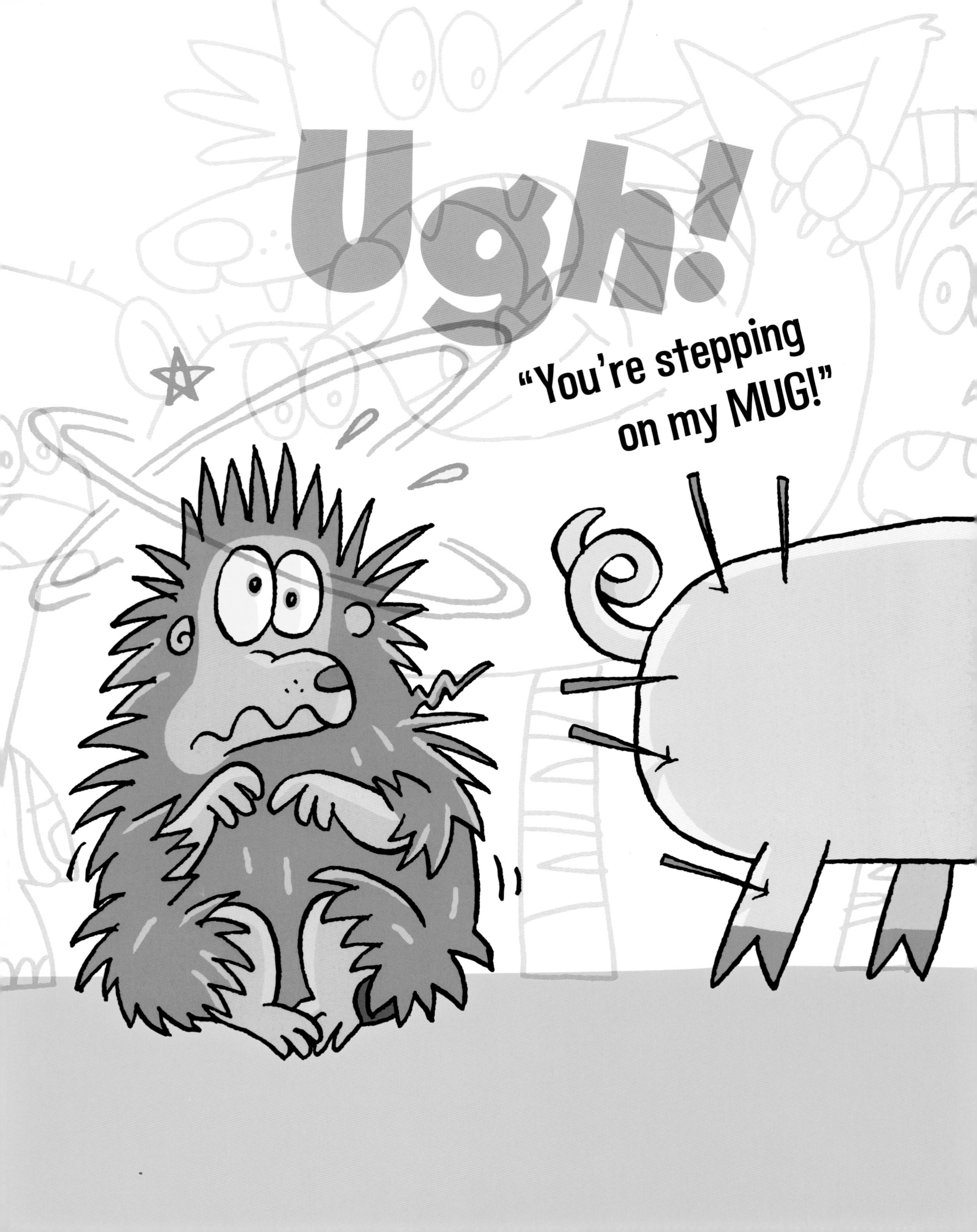
Ugh!
"You're stepping on my MUG!"

said the **swine** to the **chimpanzee.**

Afterword

So it happened that my husband, Adolph Green, and our two children lived on Central Park West . . . and I still do. The Central Park Zoo, the nation's oldest public zoo, was one of our real hangouts. All the animals were behind bars and in cramped spaces.

In the 1970s, a movement began to change the look of zoos. Old exhibits were converted into more open spaces that attempted to mimic the animals' natural habitats. Moats and fences replaced cages.

It took a while for these changes to come to the Central Park Zoo, but in 1998 . . . hooray . . . the Central Park Zoo was transformed! It was larger, freer flowing, and the animals, from the smallest gnu to the biggest bear, sported smiles and looked like they were having a swell life.

Now I'm certainly not going to say that Adolph's song, *What's New At the Zoo?*, influenced the entire animal kingdom . . . BUT . . . BUT . . . though written for fun . . . the words "Let us out! Let us out!" did not fall on deaf ears. People listened.

So go to zoos...love animals...and read this book to them!

Phyllis Newman

New York City
July, 2011